SHORT, SHARP SNACKS:

Fifteen Flash & One Short Story

by Nina Kiriki Hoffman

COPYRIGHTS PAGE

Kiriki Press, P.O. Box 10858, Eugene, Oregon 97440 U.S.A.

All stories previously published in the estimable *Daily Science Fiction*.

"While Memory Holds a Seat" © 2013 by Nina Kiriki Hoffman. Originally published in *Daily Science Fiction* 21 June 2013.

"What Remains" © 2018 by Nina Kiriki Hoffman. Originally published in *Daily Science Fiction* 15 June 2018.

"A Hundred Babies" © 2017 by Nina Kiriki Hoffman. Originally published in *Daily Science Fiction* 24 November 2017.

"Simon Says" © 2014 by Nina Kiriki Hoffman. Originally published in *Daily Science Fiction* 27 October 2014.

"The God of Rugs"© 2013 by Nina Kiriki Hoffman. Originally published in *Daily Science Fiction* 30 October 2018.

"Spring Again" © 2016 by Nina Kiriki Hoffman. Originally published in *Daily Science Fiction* 11 November 2016.

"Boy Seeds" © 2011 by Nina Kiriki Hoffman. Originally published in *Daily Science Fiction* 14 February 2011.

Table of Contents

While Memory Holds a Seat

Give us your sky for two hours and we'll fill it with story-telling spectres! That's one of the pitches we use for our traveling troupe, Wide Sky Theater. We ride the skip nodes bringing cultcha to everybody, or so we tell ourselves and each other, and then we sometimes snicker, sometimes bicker, sometimes laugh loud and long, and our new cast members, they really believe it, those wonderful naifs.

Our ship was on the way to a fringe planet called Streak. All seven of the cast and crew had gathered in the central room for a strategy discussion.

We were all cast and crew both, and we all pitched in on styling our ship, *Big Bertha*, to suit our needs and personalities. Every other chamber in *Bertha* connected to the central room, which was foamed and carpeted on every surface. Most of its furniture consisted of cushions, some firm and many squashy, in jewel colors. If the ship's gravity shifted, which it had been known to do capriciously, our pillows floofed on us instead of whacking us. This said nothing of what we did to one another. We had all learned how to land.

The scent of my daughter Verna's plum lamb casserole carried everywhere, roasted meat and sweet mingled. Verna, in lavender tunic and stained apron, leaned against the wall beside the open galley door. She had her father's dark beauty, a little softened by my generous body shape. It was almost suppertime, so this meeting would be short.

I sat against a wall near my cabin door, knitting long narrow leaves of Philloland spicebrush into a matrix of wooly cinnamon-colored yarn. I wasn't sure what would come from my fingers. A snood for Caliban, perhaps. Lately I had been surprising myself; the turquoise strands I had knitted with crackle nesting strips had turned into a strangle rope instead of the necklace I thought I'd been making for my granddaughter.

"Streak has been out of the trading mainstream for a couple of centuries," said Captain Mike, who that day was dressed like a fantasy pirate in a big-sleeved shirt, billowing pantaloons, and boots. We all borrowed from the costume closet anytime we pleased, which lent a welcome variety to our days. Mike's head sported wild waves of grizzled red hair; his bushy beard was a stripy mix of red and white. His face was wide across and short from chin to temple; he looked like a Japanese demon when he grinned and showed all his teeth. You saw that face above you in the sky, you could read every thought as it crossed his mind. Mike made a wonderful villain. "Nobody knows how far they've twisted away from galactic normal. We're going to want something basic. Universal."

"The hero's journey," said Tiller, the youngest and newest member of our company, a woodsy boy we'd found on a backwater world, anxious to rid himself of every speck of home planet dust.

I remembered that ancient urgency. I thought of the little wooden box of dirt I'd picked up last time we landed on Found. Sometimes I opened that box to stir the dirt and sniff it, catching the faintest whiff of my childhood, summer star-catching parties in the gather wallow, our hair plastered to our heads with fine warm mud as we slipped and slid amongst each other, streaking for falling bits of brightness catapulted from back porches by our parents.

Tiller longed to play heroes, but so far made do with sidekick parts.

"The time is out of joint," said Leandro, usually our male lead. Dark-skinned and bright-eyed, he slouched low in his chair, doing his usual imitation of a pre-rigor corpse. He wore a simple brown body stocking, being a man of great laziness when not on stage. You could pass him in a street or bazaar or spaceport bar and never look twice, such was his gift for disappearing when he was not using his other gifts. When he was on stage, he electrified, and counted it a bad night if he didn't get fifteen varied propositions after a play. "O, cursed spite, that ever I was born to set it right."

"Not Hamlet again," said Priss. She was a square-jawed, strong-featured woman, olive-skinned and silver-haired, who could play queen or villain with equal grace. She was my granddaughter. And she was blackmailing me.

She stared across the room at me. "It's Rose's turn to take the lead," she said, in that sharp voice that always cut me a little. "I vote we do Beauty and the Beast. And Rose plays Belle."

I dropped three stitches and two long leaves.

"I second that," said Fasha, our strong and slender moon child. Androgynous, she could play almost anything. She was also our makeup artist, so skillful she could turn us into each other, and once did so to celebrate Mask Day on Gilliland. "Rose, it's been an age since you've played a lead."

Most of them could not remember the last time I'd played a lead. Verna had been a baby. Verna's father, Basim, had been one of us, a lead more charismatic than Leandro, and always, always beautiful, in private and in public. I had been so much younger then. I was never beautiful, but my face had character, I told myself. We were doing actual live theater on a portable stage back then, none of this throwing giant images of ourselves into the sky, where every tiny detail was visible unless Fasha covered it with maquillage.

On stage, I could project, and people responded to my facial expressions. Mostly in those days I played happy women. I beamed in my toad-ugly way that was somehow endearing.

I had been happy. Basim had picked me, and I could barely believe it. Once in a while, in that tender corner of my secret self that believed I could be other people, I heard him when he called me his glorious fountain of earthly delights, his beautiful glimpse of paradise. Those tiny moments, stitched together, gave me the strength to play women I didn't believe I could ever be: the Beauties who tamed beasts, the shapeshifters who cast off their swan feathers to emerge princesses, the high-class girls who could trade witty lines with Basim's handsome lords and princes. We took our shows on a skip route that included twelve planets, and each time we returned where we had been before, our audiences grew.

Then I got pregnant with Jibril, and while I was too big to play and only acted as wardrobe mistress and makeup artist, Basim grew closer to our new ingenue, Cleo, and I lost my magic. After I gave birth to my boy and lost the extra weight, Basim pretended to love only me again, or perhaps he truly did love me. He was an easy man to believe; he spoke so beautifully.

When I got pregnant with Verna, though, he left the ship on Hitherto and never came back. Captain Mike said he had been killed in one of the bars near the spaceport. I didn't let myself check the newsflow or the incident reports, or even Basim's datacache in the Interweb, where his life story was automatically updated anytime anyone mentioned him anywhere. I told myself I believed what Captain Mike had told me, and we moved on, and found other players, and I played aunts and nurses and dotty grandmothers and sidekicks and mothers, older sisters, and occasionally villains.

I flew our ship, and I maintained the costumes and cooked, and taught my daughter to cook, and here we were, waiting to eat her plum lamb casserole once we had settled on our next play.

"I couldn't possibly," I said, imagining my giant face across the sky, that rough-featured face playing Belle. I no longer really acted in anything, unless they needed someone in the background or I could wear a mask. I took Juvena so that my bones would stay elastic, and it kept my face relatively wrinkle-free, but I still had the same peasant features I had always believed saved me from beauty.

"You will," said Priss. She tapped her finger on her right temple, reminding me that she knew what I had never told anyone: that I was responsible for her Uncle Jibril's death.

Jibril grew up on the ship, every year more the image of his father. He had had no interest in play acting, and since he liked to work with his hands most, I had apprenticed him at sixteen to a jewelry maker on Diala, where they make the most marvelous and expensive show pieces. They train metal to follow the curves and curls of living plants, shape jewels to capture the essence of the elements, clear as water, brilliant as flame, dark as caves, fragile as bubbles.

He caught up with me on the skip route six years later. He had pinged me, and only me, on the

Interweb, saying he wanted to see me alone. *Bertha* put in at Diala, where the atmosphere is thin and the night is dark and clear. The people live under clear-glassed skies, and the air always smells of incense from the many altars everywhere.

We were doing one of the more obscure Shakespeare plays. Verna had a big part in it, and I played no one, so I went off during the performance to find Jibril. I met him in the Viewport Restaurant.

My son stood at the rail in the dome that looked out over the shuttle dock, where little ships rode elevators into orbit. He looked so much like his father. He brought me a tiara he had crafted himself, a sinuous silver weave of vines with water-drop rounded jewels caught in their tendrils, and set it on my head, saying, "For my beautiful mother." His voice had matured, too, into that rich, deep tone his father had used, so mellow and musical he could convince you a moon's reflection was the moon.

"It's much too fine for me," I told my son. Such splendor belonged on a head more glorious than mine. I tried to take it off, but he stayed my hand.

"I made it for you," he said, "for you alone. This is what I see when I think of you."

He sounded so like his father it tore through the patches I had slapped on Basim's betrayal and opened again the crack in my heart. I pushed away from him, this loving image of my beloved, and watched, horrified, as my push sent him over the rail--so slowly I could have rushed forward and snatched him back, I knew I could, only I lunged for him and I, too, was caught in a sticky snag of time that slowed everything and gave me forever to see him fall to the inward curve of the dome's base, a hundred meters below.

My lunge took me to the rail, which cracked

against my ribs. I embraced the rush of pain. All I
wanted to do was slide over the rail into the endless
open, find my own finish down there beside the
crumpled body of my son, but others pulled me
back.

Someone took me to a med facility, and they
fastgrew my crackling bones back. Some witnesses
told police it was deliberate and others said it was
an accident. The viewcams showed that I had turned
away while I pushed, that he had skidded as he
reached for me, and my reluctant but compelled
testimony under truthstim said it was an accident, so
they let me go, even though I wanted to go
nowhere.

I had nowhere else to go but back to *Bertha*. So
there I ended up, in a walking zombie state, and
Captain Mike put me to bed, asking no questions.

I spent the next three skips not stirring from my
bed except to use the head. Verna and Captain Mike
made me drink nourishment; I did not care enough
to stop them. They thought I had caught some
Dialan parasite the ship's doc couldn't diagnose.

Eventually I had to let go of my grief or find a
way to beat my head in. I let the details of the
everyday lift me away from my memories, and
Captain Mike never took us to Diala again.

I hadn't known what Mike and Verna did with
the tiara Jibril had made me, not until a week ago,
when Priss found it in a small compartment I didn't
even remember my cabin contained. She looked at
it and recognized Jibril's sigil; he had sent me some
of his apprentice work earlier, and those I had kept
with my other small personal pieces of jewelry.
Priss always liked to play with them when she was a
child, and she had begged Verna and me for stories

about Basim and Jibril.

Somehow she knew the rest of this particular story once she saw the tiara. Perhaps she had done what Mike and Verna hadn't, checked his datacache on the Interweb and learned how and where he died. And now, hateful child, she was ready to force me into something that would break my heart again.

Belle. Beauty.

"I will play the Beast," I said.

"A reversal!" said Fasha. "Captain Mike can play Belle!"

We all looked at each other, and most of us laughed.

Mike and I stared at each other. Belle was the last lead I had played, before Jibril was a bump in my belly, while Basim was still with the company. To play Belle to Basim's Beast had left me bubbling with hidden mirth. I had crafted the mask that made him ugly; wearing it, he could roar and scare all the children in the audience.

Each time Basim transformed into a handsome prince at the end, I felt again my amazement that he had found me beautiful enough to love.

"Play Belle, Rose," said Leandro. "I've seen holos of your old productions. You were wonderful."

"Play Belle, Mother," said Verna. "I've never seen you sky act in a lead role."

"Play Belle," said Tiller. "I didn't even know you acted."

"Play Belle," Mike said. "Call back your lost selves. They've lived in those graves on other planets too long, Rosie."

Then I knew he had known about Jibril all along. In his eyes I saw no condemnation, only concern. I glanced at Priss. She couldn't threaten me with exposure if Mike already knew.

I wanted to be Belle again. I took Jibril's last gift to me out of my yarn bag and stared down into the eyes of its jewels. "Yes."

§§§

What Remains

I was the only one alive when the Picti found our shipwrecked shuttle pod.

Sang, Tadala, and I had jumped through the wrong skip node on our way back to the mother ship. We landed on a planet we found on the other side of the uncharted node. Our rescue beacon probably couldn't reach anyone we knew. The pod had supplies and air for only five days.

All of us offered our bodies to each other as we lay dying, and none of us accepted the sacrifice. We were all vegetarians, and the air would run out soon anyway. We lay together, holding hands, staring at the mandala on the ceiling as life left us. Our only comfort lay in knowing we were with the ones we loved. Perhaps in the next life we would find each other again.

The Picti arrived in a rush of bad planetary air as they opened the pod door. I had hardly any awareness left, but coughing and choking woke me enough to see, with weeping eyes, that we were surrounded by silver, pulsing mounds that moved. A cool pseudopod touched my face, then covered it. My skin sizzled, and then I could breathe again.

I lost my last rags of consciousness then.

When I woke, I was surrounded by me. Three me's looked down at me. None of us wore clothing.

I lay on something soft that was also the floor of a very small chamber. The room was roundish, coated with a rough, moist, red-pink substance that felt under my hands and bare back like the surface of a tongue. The ceiling was very low. I felt like I was inside a giant, toothless mouth. Its breath smelled like lemons and curry. Soft yellow light shone from small bumps here and there in the red stuff.

The three faces above me, all mine, looked worried, though to different degrees. They were all too close to me.

"What?" I said, and reached up to touch a face. It leaned closer to let me pat it. I fingered its lips, its nose, its mustache, so familiar, though I'd never seen myself from the outside like this before. It blinked its dark eyes.

"Have I died? How are there more of me?"

"Milumili," it said, its voice my very pitch and timbre, its words nonsense.

I fumbled for my utility belt, where I had a universal translator, though why I couldn't understand myself was a mystery.

My utility belt was gone, like everything else I owned. I looked at the nearest me's chest and found differences: the slash of scar from a misfired laser near my left nipple was missing. None of the white scratch scars from my childhood tiger playmate shone in the brown skin of his shoulders.

Someone else pushed into the chamber, crowding us all even closer, close enough to taste each other's breaths. This one had the face of my beloved, Sang. I held out my arms to her, and she squeezed past the me's and held her arms out to me. But she did not come all the way into my embrace. I struggled up and pulled her into a hug, wondering if this was a strange afterlife.

Her arms came around my torso after a brief hesitation, and then, somehow, skin to skin with my beloved, I knew this was not my beloved. Though she breathed and felt and smelled like my beloved, the one I loved was not there. We had no ease in our embrace. It was the touch of strangers.

I sagged against the stubby red floor. It squirmed beneath me. I closed my eyes and lay with the mystery. I realized I no longer felt hunger or thirst, nor hot, nor cold. I must be dead.

The second time I woke, Tadala was beside me in the small red room. His beloved dark face wore no expression. He studied my face as though he knew me not.

"Tadala?" I said, though I knew this was not my beloved.

He touched my chest, then my face. He looked closely at me, then held up his hand with its lovely long fingers, and nodded toward it. I studied it. It had none of the small scars Tadala had acquired while welding, and all its fingernails were intact. As I watched, the hand melted into a silver blob.

I gasped and reached up to touch it. Surface tension held it in a shape, but it gave beneath my fingers, not quite as liquid as quicksilver, nor as hard as bread dough. Tadala's serious face studied me as I grasped the silver bulb and squeezed it. It bulged out between my fingers. When I opened my hand, it coalesced again into an orb. The silver traveled up Tadala's arm to his shoulder, then started across his chest, until only his head remained, surrounded by silver.

Then I knew my true beloveds were dead, and I was still alive, with people who could look like us.

"Who are you?" I asked as loss opened a dark chasm in my chest, and hope fell into it.

The silver sent a pseudopod toward me. It held my utility belt. I took the belt and opened the pouch where I kept the universal translator. This was an undocumented species, one I'd never seen in the galactic cooperative. Its language profile would not be in the translator yet, but the translator worked partly in the future, looking ahead to when we would understand each other, if understanding was possible. I held the translator out, and the silver being with Tadala's face touched it as I touched it. I tapped the translator on and said, "Who are you, please?"

The translator vibrated, then vibrated again, and a voice came out of it, the null voice the translator supplied to those who used nonvocal speech. "We are Picti," it said. "We wish to encounter more of your species. How do we get where your others are?"

"How is it you take the shapes of me and my friends?" I asked.

"We have tasted you. It is how we learn new species. We had to adjust you to live in our atmosphere. We understand some solids dislike any shift. We apologize for altering you, but it was necessary to sustain life."

I closed my eyes and opened my mind. Before our shuttle pod limped to a landing on that planet, we had used its faltering equipment to scan stars, and located some we knew. They were half a galaxy away, an impossible distance by straight-line travel, and our access to the node webs had died.

I could tell the Picti the direction in which to find humans, but I knew nothing about their mode of travel or their intentions toward us.

I abandoned all hope that I would ever see another of my own kind.

When I opened my eyes, I looked up into the face of Sang, framed by her long black hair. Her eyes held the gentle kindness that defined her.

"We are too far from home ever to return," I

told the Picti who wore the form of my beloved. "You will have to learn only from me."

She touched my face with cool fingertips. "It is a start," she said.

§§§

A Hundred Babies

When Father Robert stepped outside the rectory Monday morning to visit the pauper's grave where he prayed every day, he found the cemetery playing host to scores of babies.

They were all different races, most wrapped in brightly hued gowns that, he hoped, kept out the chill of morning mist; fog lay in the low grounds of the cemetery, with baby parts emerging from it, baby parts he hoped were attached to whole babies rather than being dismemberments. The babies were quiet and self-absorbed, none laughing, crying, or speaking—none that he could see in obvious distress. All seemed older than infants, though not by much.

Sun struck through the mist, outlining the old oak trees with gold as the sky lightened. Father Robert blinked several times, but the babies did not vanish.

He stood on the threshold of his dwelling and prayed God would give him direction. He had never spent time with babies or children, other than Sunday school instruction he'd tried once to give to a roomful of six-year-olds who did not choose to pay attention to him. Now he left the instruction of the young ones to Elaine and Dicey, grandmothers with strong faith backgrounds and lots of experience with children, women who did not back away from little hands and unanswerable questions.

Where did these babies come from? Why send them to me? Father Robert wondered.

The Bible verse "Take care of my sheep" came to him. An answer?

Father Robert went to the nearest grave and

knelt in the wet grass near a baby in a purple gown. It sat up, looking around. It sucked its thumb. It stared up at him.

"Maybe I should take you inside and call for help," Father Robert said.

The child popped its thumb out of its mouth and held its arms out to Father Robert. He drew in a breath, then lifted the baby off the grave of Hilda Ravensong, dead these thirty-odd years. He held it at arms' length, supporting it under its arms, and stared into its face, paralyzed by indecision. The baby reached out to him. Hesitating, he brought it closer. It hugged him around the neck. It smelled sour and wild, and it felt warm.

"You are distressed," he said, even though the baby did not seem upset.

Spontaneous acts of affection were not in Father Robert's repertoire. Everyone watched priests for misbehavior these days; better to touch no one at all.

Should he pull the infant away from him? What if someone walked by outside the cemetery's low wall and saw? He closed his eyes and asked God for help.

God said, "Embrace the child."

Father Robert's arms crept up and wrapped around the baby. A cascade of memories and dreams flooded his mind: his father's hug when Robert was a boy and had fallen from the oak tree by the barn; the shock of the fall, the remedy of his father's arms; his father's leather, Old Spice, and sweat scent, the heat of life; his father's power to make everything better.

Another memory came, from later in his life, when he heard God's call and chose the priesthood after a long night of thinking about all the possibilities his choice would take away from him: the chance to love someone other than Jesus, the chance to marry and father his own children and take care of them. He had made himself picture that alternative life—wife, two children, a cozy house in the suburbs with green lawn and fruit trees in the back yard. He lived there in his imagination, then asked himself if the call to God was stronger. And, considering everything, it was.

The families he had counseled through their complicated conflicts flashed through his mind.

And then he thought nothing, just felt the warm child in his embrace, heard the child's breathing near his ear, smelled the slightly sour milky scent of its breath and body.

The child pushed away and gurgled something at him. He set it on its feet. It laughed and fell on its bottom, still looking into his eyes.

The mist had melted, revealing babies on graves. Old graves, fresh graves, graves of people he had known and people who had died before he came to this church. Graves people cared for, and graves of people no one remembered. Every grave in this small cemetery had a baby on it.

All the babies had noticed him now. All crawled toward him, gurgling and babbling to each other as they converged. They held arms up to him. He hugged them one by one. When he had embraced them, they crawled off.

He did not keep count. As he circled them with his arms, thought left him; all he had was this mission, giving each child affection and warmth. The sun strengthened. He was hot in his black cassock, and he felt the heat on the bald spot on his head where a tonsure might be were he a monk.

"Father Robert!"

The child in his arms loosened her hold on his neck, and he gently set her down and looked up, dazed, wondering how many more babies waited for a hug. The leader of the church altar guild, Karen Sanderson, an elderly, silver-haired, trim woman clad in a dark blue dress and silver tennis shoes, stared down at him, her large tapestry handbag clutched to her chest.

"Ga," said a baby. Father Robert looked down at the final child in front of him, a brown-skinned cherub with black curls and a wide smile. She wore a yellow gown. He smiled at her and picked her up, his arms forming into a now-practiced embrace, holding her firmly but not too tight, supporting her. She pressed her ear to his chest, gripped his clerical collar, and closed her eyes.

"What are you doing?" Karen asked.

He let out a long, contented sigh. The child stretched up and kissed his neck, then pushed away from him. He set her down, then looked around.

The babies had vanished, all except the one he had just finished hugging. She crawled toward the oak trees. He got to his feet, brushing off his cassock, and watched her, wondering if he should go after her or let her go.

"Father Robert!"

He glanced at Karen, eyebrows up. When he looked back, the last child was gone.

"What on Earth is going on here?" Karen said.

He didn't think he could explain anything that had just happened. His arms were tired, and his chest was awash in warm contentment.

"What was—?" Karen looked around. "Where did they go?"

"I had a vision," Father Robert said. "God gave me a gift." He opened his arms.

Karen frowned at him, set her handbag on the ground, and stiffly walked into a hug. He held her gently, with the strength and skill of a hundred hugs.

§§§

Simon Says

I don't know how many of us are in this head. I just got here, and I'm ready to leave.

We have to take turns using the eyes, face, and mouth. Simon the repeater has been telling me the rules. The core personality gets to hog the eye time, because she's the one with a job, and we need that job if we want to have our own apartment. Otherwise we'd have to live with her parents, and whenever that happens, it gets more crowded in here.

Simon says he moved in when Core was tasked with saying, "I will not touch myself there" a thousand times. Core did the first fifteen times, but every time she stuttered, the father pressed a lit cigarette into her arm. Core can't say the word "touch" without a stutter, but Simon can. Touch touch touch.

Toby has a high pain threshold. Kevin does the jobs that need us not to pay attention to what's going on around us. Annie takes care of things that involve blood, wounds, medical treatments, or body emergencies. Core throws up when faced with that stuff.

Me, I can talk to the little kids in the daycare where Core works without scaring them. Simon says I'm the fifth person Core developed just for that, because the other alters keep telling us what else Core knows, and we get polluted, and the toddlers can tell.

Thor is in charge of social interactions with adults who aren't Core's parents. Thor likes me, or says he does. Thor told Simon to stop talking to me. Simon is the main alter who pollutes people by telling them things.

Simon can't help himself. He has to repeat, whether he's in charge of the eyes or not.

"You're killing Eliza," Thor says when Simon tells me things. Thor shows me the head's graveyard. Shadowy corpses lie strewn across a gray ground, all their details hard to make out except the sticky labels on their chests. HELLO, MY NAME IS: Bob. Helena. Alexander.

Some of them died twisted, in pain, maimed or mutilated. Others look unmarked.

Simon says, "Stop showing her that, Thor. You're killing her. Or giving her ideas."

It's my turn with the eyes. I kneel next to a weeping child clutching a broken doll on a block-scattered yellow linoleum floor. The shrieks, laughter, and chatter of other children sound through an open door to a green and sunlit world.

"It's all right, honey. It's all right," I say, stroking my hand down her soft, pink, unscarred arm. "I can fix your doll." One of the boys tore its arms off.

Electrum, the keeper of memories, shows me a stack of broken dolls, and how none of them ever got really fixed. They got stuck back together with tape, or repainted, or they had glass eye transplants, or doll socks pulled up over their charred feet, but they never felt safe after that first "accident." They lost their sparkle.

Kissy, she's the master of fake sparkle.

I ease the doll from the child's grip, then the doll's arms. "She's not really hurt," I say. "Look. They go right back in." I pop the arms back into place.

Matt's the do-unto-others person, and most of what he does gets us into trouble. He wants our mouth to yell at the little girl, "Stop your soggy yammering or I'll give you something to cry about!" Matt has gotten us fired three times.

I keep my mouth shut to prevent Matt's words from getting out.

"All better," I say, showing the little girl that the doll's arms work now.

She breaks into a smile, kisses my cheek, and runs outside. I lose my turn behind the eyes.

Electrum tells me stories about kisses that hurt.

I'd rather talk to Simon.

§§§

The God of Rugs

My mother worshipped the god of rugs, which gave her peculiar powers, and gave me the conviction that I needed to find a god of my own.

"Well, Karen," Mom said, "so glad you finally decided to visit."

"You make it so inviting." I sat on the cabbage-rose printed couch, from which, to be fair, she had recently vacuumed the pet hair. Today's air freshener scent was a cloying version of patchouli. Mom's favorite Persian rug had a grip around both my ankles. I knew if I didn't tread carefully, I'd be stuck in Mom's living room for hours—maybe overnight, if she was feeling mean or her dementia kicked in.

Her collection of ceramic owls in various sizes, colors, and states of arousal stared at me from the knickknack shelves and the occasional tables.

"Are you saying you'd stay here longer than five minutes if I didn't take extreme measures to keep you here?" Mom asked.

"Probably not, but I'd come by more often if you didn't scare me so much."

"I see. Well, I think I should just make the most of this visit, since I don't know when you'll be back. Would you like some tea?"

"Will you let me go to the bathroom?"

"Considering what happened last time, I think not."

"No tea, then," I said.

"No tea, thank you," she corrected.

I considered not repeating after her, but the last time I did that, a throw rug had crept up my body and wrapped around my lower face. I had breathed in a lot of dirt and dog hair. It gave me hives. "No tea, thank you," I said in as snotty a tone as I dared.

"How about cookies?" Mom asked.

"The lemon ones? Sure," I said. Then, remembering my manners, "That would be lovely."

She put two lemon cookies on a plate and set them on the lion-legged coffee table in front of me.

"Thank you." I ate one and wrapped the other in a napkin for later. No telling how long she'd keep me here, and I wasn't sure her hospitality would extend to supper.

"So how's Jason?" Mom asked.

The rug was licking my ankle. I didn't want to speculate with what. It had never done that before. "Who?"

"Your fianc," she said.

My fantasy boyfriend. Oh, dear. "We broke up." I was tired of supplying her with details of fictional dates, but the instant I said it, I knew it was a mistake.

"You were too good for him," she said.

The rug slipped my shoes off my feet. It felt furry and a little rough as it caressed my toes. Warm heaviness pooled in my belly. "Sure," I said, my voice whispery.

"Karen!"

I blinked and straightened. The rug was creeping up my calves. It felt warm and weirdly muscular for fabric. "Mom, I need to leave now," I said. I kind of wished she would leave the room.

"You just got here," she said. "I want to know where you're going to meet a good young man. You can't live your life alone. A person needs a helpmeet. Have you tried online dating?"

"Have you?" Dad left her seventeen years ago, and she'd been alone since, aside from the rug god thing. "I hear OkCupid is good." I wiggled my toes. The rug tightened on them.

Mom sat back in her floral armchair. She stared past my head. "No," she said. "I haven't. I wonder." She set down her teacup and saucer and headed out of the room. I heard faint keystroking from her study next door.

The rug made its move. It wrapped me up like I was a dead body about to be carried out to someone's car trunk for disposal. I never knew corpses could have so much fun. That it was happening on my mom's ugly couch, with her in the next room, made it much creepier and more intense.

By the time the rug unrolled me, it was dark. My watch wasn't on my wrist anymore, so I couldn't tell what time it was. Mom was still typing away in the next room. I pulled myself back together, but I couldn't find my peacock-blue underwear, until I took a good look at the rug, which had a new line of color around its edge. I grabbed my shoes and purse and tiptoed out of the living room, then made my escape.

I wondered if the god of clothes would grant me powers if I worshipped him or her. Clothes could be intimate, and clothes could be armor. I composed my first prayer.

§§§

Spring Again

I hate spring.

My best friend Bran and I were sitting in his red Mini Cooper Hardtop two-door, parked out in the wetlands west of town, looking out at the cool, cloudy night sky and listening to the mating calls of frogs.

The seasonal imperative our species lives with says spring is the time to mate and grow big with the next generation. I only have to do this if one of the males catches me, though. If I would just stop putting out pheromones, I could hide for the month I'm fertile, and I wouldn't have to lay the damned eggs every year. I wouldn't have to decide whether to kill my mate. Some of them deserve death for the way they treat me when I'm in their mating grip, but some don't. If I leave them alive, though, they're so wasted after the biggest event in their lives that someone has to take care of them for several years while they recover their strength. Not a job any female of our species relishes.

The chorus of frog croaks had started earlier this year than ever before, way before frost stopped edging the night with lace. The air was cold and full of water vapor, and the first pollen particles from trees, and the smell of plant life waking and rising. I had already begun to grow scent-emitting tendrils in my hair, though they hadn't started spilling pheromones yet. I snipped them out every morning, though that hurt. I could never find all of them.

"Just let me do it," said Bran. "Let me fertilize you. I think this might be the year I mature. I've been getting feelings I don't understand, and you look different to me, more juicy or something. You smell appetizing."

I sighed. Bran was ten years older than I was, and I had hoped he'd never grow up. Males took a long time to achieve sexual maturity among our kind. I knew some guys who were eighty years old and hadn't gotten there yet. I liked the immature ones. They were no kind of threat, and could be good friends. It was the crop who developed secondary sexual characteristics with the advent of spring I had to watch out for. "Bran. Not you. Please. Not yet."

He edged his hand under mine on my thigh, and I curled my fingers around it. We listened to the frogs. The outside edge of Bran's hand was forming the hard, knobbed ridge a male needed to grip and paralyze a female. He was right. He was growing up.

If he matured this year, he would have to mate, if he could track down a female. Then he'd probably die. Especially if it were someone other than me. Most of my mates had been men I didn't know and didn't care about; there were always plenty to choose from, so many it was impossible to avoid them all. I actually flew to the Galapagos one year, hoping none of our kind would be there, but six turned up when my tendrils activated. That year, I killed my mate, and only two of my hundred offspring survived to pupate. They were my least favorite children.

"Even if you kill me," Bran said. "I want it to be you."

Better me than anybody else. My best friends were female members of my own species. We could never tell humans why we hid for three months every spring. We couldn't let ourselves be seen when our bellies stretched to their fullest, because humans did not change that much in their pregnancies, even those bearing multiple embryos. We hid in the geothermal caves together when we were at our biggest, so we could lay the eggs in the warm pits where they had the best chance to survive. We sometimes fed each other's broods after they hatched. One didn't get involved with the larval stages, just fed them once a week and watched them fight each other for survival. They couldn't think properly until after they pupated, so the titanic losses of most of them didn't hurt very much.

Bran had attended me through five years of egg laying, bringing me food and water while I was immobilized, keeping me clean and comfortable, or as comfortable as a person can be when she's almost twice her normal size and can't rise to her feet. So many body structures change for that horrible time. I would spend all of it knocked out if I could.

He was the best helper I'd had since I'd reached sexual maturity eight years ago. But if he was mature this year, I'd lose him, one way or another. If I refused him, his seasonal imperative would send him after someone else. Most of us lost our minds after mating and laying, so furious and ecstatic we were, so pumped full of the hormones of completion and elation. Common knowledge said we were not responsible for what we did in the mad time.

Or maybe it was tradition, established on behalf of the Mad Mothers of the Autubiakishta. We said we lost our minds then. I had never discussed it with my friends, but my mind was not so far away I couldn't get back into it in those times. I kept my mind, and I killed my mates anyway, because that was what we did.

I had never mated with a friend.

Bran's hand was warm under mine. He smelled like wood smoke. I didn't want him to find someone else and die under her palps.

"All right," I said.

I rubbed my fingers along the hard, bumpy edge of his hand and felt already the flush of arousal under my skin, though neither of us were ready for the act. The frog chorus swelled, and I looked through the darkness at his face. His lips parted, and the proboscis of a mature male slipped out from under his tongue. He leaned toward me and ran the soft tip of it along my jaw. I closed my eyes and ingested his scent, wood smoke, crushed rosemary leaves, and sour milk. Delicious.

"Thanks, whatever comes of this," he whispered after we had tasted each other. Tendrils writhed in my hair. I smelled my own attraction, and it excited me. He wrapped his arms around me and stimulated the nodes behind my ears. A tide rose in me, though my egg sac was still shrunken and small.

Maybe this year would be different.

§§§

Boy Seeds

Most of Noma's study friends were growing their own boys with the new Vampire, Werewolf, or Wizard Seed kits. Her best friend Celestine invited Noma to the grow room in her family compartment to take a look at a half-grown vamp.

"I specified the golden hair and dark eyebrows," Celestine said, "but he opened his eyes for the first time yesterday, and they're this weird greenish color. I ordered sky blue. Skies were blue, right?"

"They look that way in the history holos," Noma said. Noma glanced sideways into Celestine's eyes, which were the blue they had always called sky.

Celestine turned toward Noma, and reflected grow-light flared in her eyes. "What?" she asked.

Noma shook her head and rubbed sweat from her forehead. The wet air was thick with the smell of grow matrix, acrid and sour. The grow room sweltered under too-bright lights; its dark red walls were beaded with water. It was small, a standard-sized room for growing things that didn't need a lot of space. Noma and Celestine barely fit into it with the boy; the tending station was designed for one person. "Can't you turn on the blower?"

"Not while he's growing. He needs this atmosphere," Celestine said.

Noma squatted and stared at the naked boy rooted in the growth matrix. He was still in his chrysalis, a membrane containing him, binding his arms to his sides, and cloaking him in a glistening layer of cloud. His face had fae eyebrows, straight lines that started at the bridge of the nose and aimed above the ears, like an interrupted V. The features were perfect, just like the vamps in the trancies.

Noma leaned closer, staring into that perfect face with its slender nose and full red lips. The rows of dark eyelashes fluttered. The eyes opened. They were larger than human eyes, almost anime eye-size, and they were a strange pea-paste green. She leaned away from him, bumping Celestine. "Eww. Did you buzz the dispensary?" Noma asked.

"They said they'd send someone to collect and replace him if I wanted, but I'm kind of curious now. Once he hatches, the warranty expires, though, and I'm stuck with him. I think I have a couple more days to decide. What do you think, Nome? Want one like this? Or are you going to be a traitor and go to the wolf or wizard side?"

"You know," said Noma, "I don't think I want anything that's going to bite me. Did you see Betula's neck in soshe class yesterday? Owie." She wiped more sweat off her forehead. Her sleeve wicked the liquid away, but that didn't relieve the heat.

"You don't want to design your own, do you? Crayola did that, and look what she ended up with—that green hairless water thingie that slobbered constantly and couldn't converse."

"I'll use the Help tools," Noma said. The vampire was staring at her. His lips parted, and a pointed tongue flicked across the upper one, slicking the inner side of the chrysalis membrane. "Ewwie. I'd buzz the dispensary, Cel. Eww."

Noma stopped in the station's communal room and plugged into the general dispensary. "Boy time," her account reminded her.

"Shut. Up," she said. But really, that was why she had plugged in. All the girls her age were experimenting with boy-making. If she kept ignoring the option, it would trigger attention from the regulators. She'd had that experience already when she was five and wouldn't play with the mini-humans. She was supposed to design family groupings for them and make them procreate, but she couldn't get herself to tackle the project. All the other girls finished playing with their mini-humans in half a year, but Noma had to do community service for nine months, cleaning out the hydroponics lines, which, as one of her mothers noted, wasn't exactly equivalent service or training.

Noma hadn't opted for a pet at eight, either, not until the regulators sent her scary messages. Then she got a snake, because it was very low maintenance. Not that any of the made-pets took much work. Still, she was glad she had picked something that didn't do or need much, something she didn't even like. Most of her friends cried when their pets had to be recycled. Noma had never bonded with the snake. Instead she had developed programs that would take care of it without her help.

Noma's three mothers had muttered about the pet project, which was supposed to train girls to take care of smaller beings in preparation for parenthood. "Teach them they can lose what they love," Mora said to the other two. "Like that's what girls need to learn at eight or nine. Why don't one of you get on the education committee so we can shift some of these policies?"

"I'm not doing it," said Anti.

"Not interested," said Ilera. "You're the one griping about it. You do it."

But of course Mora never did. Her strength lay in complaining.

Noma tapped the "order boy" glowspot on the

dispensary screen. It showed her the most popular options, including the vampires, wizards, and werewolves, right at the top. She could choose skin color, hair color, eye color, and body type, but there wasn't much choice in personalities. She pressed some options and looked at the sample model, shifted colors, rotated the image to see it from behind. She didn't like the vampire boys. The werewolf boys were even worse. The wizard boys didn't have distinguishing marks, which made her wonder. Of course, magic didn't work, so what made these boys different? She checked the specs: Higher in intuitive skills, more able with energy flow tools. Huh?

She tapped the "Vintage" button. Ten years earlier, station girls had ordered shapeshifter boys who could change into animals. Ten years before that, it had been designer skin colors. Before that, boys with varying numbers of arms and legs, even a two-headed option, which, according to the stats, had not been very popular.

All these types were still available, or she could invent her own, but she'd have to take care of what she created for a period of six months, no matter what he turned out like. She remembered Crayola's failure and shuddered.

Maybe if she were careful—

Her mother Anti joined Noma in their compartment's grow room. They both stared at the boy rising from the growth matrix. "Oh, Noma," Anti said, patting Noma's back, "you always find a way to get in trouble, don't you? I wonder whose genes are responsible for that."

"What do you mean?" Noma said, but of course, she knew. The boy she had designed looked too much like Celestine. It hadn't been so obvious in the sample. She hadn't even realized until yesterday, when he opened his eyes behind the membrane and Noma realized they were the exact color of Celestine's, blue as old Earth skies.

Anti's finger hovered over the "Abort" button. "You can always marry her later, if you still like who she is when she grows up, but if you make it this clear now—you kids are so young." She sighed. "What do you want me to do?"

"How can I kill him when he looks like that?"

"If you let him come to term, you'll have to kill him after you get to know him, and that will be worse," said Anti. "You'd be better off doing what you did with the pet assignment. Make something you won't care about. When I had to kill my boy—" Anti hung her head, her shoulders drooping. "Ilera laughed when they recycled hers, but I don't know. I think this might be—" She glanced around and noticed the ever-present monitor eyes.

There was a part of the station so private no one Noma knew had ever seen it, the monitor center, where the regulators gathered all the information from every life onboard and evaluated which way to push for a maximum-health community. Anti sighed, and said, "I think this 'make a boy, then recycle a boy' might be very bad policy."

"What did Mora do?" Noma asked.

"We didn't know her then. She was in a different school. I don't know how she handled it. She didn't keep a picture of her boy in her memory book, so I don't even know what she chose. But I think—" She stared down at the abort button. "You should be the one to press it."

Noma knelt and looked at her growing boy. He stared back, with eyes the color of Celestine's. His face had no expression; he didn't know enough to feel. Something swept through her, familiar and frustrating, a longing for something she couldn't imagine.

The station portals showed vast black sky with glowing stars, the biggest one their sun, but so far away! Sometimes she could see the planets of the system, crescents to the side of the sun, shadows as they moved across its face, small, small, unless she refocused the view and brought them closer. No matter how hard she looked, they were too far away to touch. All any of the people had was the station and whatever recorded memories the regulators would let them experience, and sometimes that wasn't enough.

She touched the membrane enclosing her boy, though all the grow instructions said you should never do that. Its surface was slick, hot, and a little sticky. A black spot grew beneath her fingertip. She jerked her hand back, dismayed, and watched the spot spread. The boy in his sheath grimaced. His mouth opened, but no sound came out.

Noma jumped up and pressed the abort button. The growth matrix parted and the boy dropped back into the vat he had grown from. It didn't hurt. All the instruction manuals said it didn't hurt creatures when they were reabsorbed. All of them said that. But his grimacing face was burned into her memory.

She turned to her mother, who hugged her tight, letting Noma bury sobs against her mother's breast. "Choose one you won't love," Anti whispered in her ear when Noma's sobs had slackened.

Noma slept first, then went back to the dispensary. She picked a vampire boy, because Celestine had a vampire boy. She closed her eyes to pick the colors and attributes, letting her finger wander over the screen without watching. The dispensary played a chime when she had finished, and she looked at what she had ordered. Dark skin, brown hair, amber eyes, compact body type. Not like anyone she knew. She pressed "select."

She knew she would end up loving him.

§§§

Test Drive

It was my turn to wear the mask, but my egg-sister Linney wouldn't give it up. She'd been wearing the mask all morning, set on Smile, and it was a test day, too. Everyone thought she was so pleased and relaxed and Earthy.

I am wretched at tests, but the mask would have helped. I flunked my Calm test that morning, scored medium low on Earth Facial Expressions, and got a fifty in grooming because I didn't know how to put on makeup. The mask has its own. Maybe I depend on that too much, even though I only get to wear the mask half the time I'm awake.

Linney didn't even need the mask. Imitating this planet's sentient life forms comes naturally to her. Some days I just want to kill her.

But that's not an option, at least not while we're training under the eyes of everybody still inside the ship, so I went to Dad Two instead and complained.

"You always do this, Morana. Play the poor-little-me card. I'm tired of taking care of you. Deal with it yourself."

"I never wanted to be human anyway," I said and rushed away before he could tell me he didn't like my attitude. I've had a bad attitude since we arrived on Earth. Nobody complained about my attitude on Zalon. Then I was the expert, and Linney was the stupid one because she wasn't used to having six arms and didn't know what to do with two of them.

In the afternoon we were going out for our first field test. Skitty was taking us to a mall, where Linney and I were supposed to wander around like North American Teenagers and see if we made contact with local life forms.

"I want that mask," I said to Linney over lunch. Skitty sat on a pod to the side, her tap pad at the ready, watching our every move.

I hate test days.

"You can't have it," Linney said. "Last time you wore it, you broke the mouth and it was stuck on Frown for two days. You've lost your mask privileges."

If I had had three more arms, I would have strangled her.

I finished eating my fimsaw, and Linney said, "You're going to have to change those teeth, or you'll flunk before we're even out the door."

I growled at her.

"That's a ten-point deduction," she said. "Humans don't have that kind of vocal range."

I ran away before Skitty could mark me down any farther. I spent the rest of lunch period in our cabin, going over the Human specs again and remolding myself to conform. If Linney got a mission before I did on this planet she would smug me to death. I had to pass.

I met Skitty and Linney at the outer lock at the appointed time.

"You look nice," Skitty said. "I like what you've done with your hair."

Linney had exactly the same hairstyle I did, long, yellow, and straight around her shoulders, held back with a blue band. I guess we'd both copied from the same model.

We climbed into the disguised scoot and drove to the mall.

The mall was a big low building like a crouching cityship. We went in an airlock and stepped into strange sensations. Sound that was sort of like music, and lots of people talking in the limited bandwidth humans use. The smells were various and strange.

Skitty herded us down the hall toward the conglomerated food outlets. Our first test was eating in public.

Linney ordered a Happy Meal. This concept always made me wince. How can a meal be happy when it is about to be consumed?

I'd studied lots of menus and even tried some of the foods, so I ordered a vanilla milkshake. It was the only thing I was sure I could keep in my primary stomach.

"That's not eating," Linney said through her perpetual smile.

I stuck a straw in my thick shake and walked away, smiling myself. Skitty paid for our food and herded us toward a table.

Linney had to manage the mouth controls in the mask to eat, whereas I could just suck on my straw and ingest, even while smiling. Skitty hadn't gotten any food. She tapped on her pad.

"Twins," said a passing human. I judged him an adolescent, even though he was as large as an adult. His dark hair stuck up in spikes and he was wearing a black T-shirt with holes torn in it and black pants with lots of chains on them. "Hey, twins! How ya doing?"

"Wanna sit?" I said, scoring points by conversing with a native. I gestured toward the fourth chair at our table.

"Awesome," he said, and sat. "Hey, my name's Palmer. What's yours?"

I couldn't remember my Earth name. "Morana. Nice to eat you, Palmer."

"Eat me!" he said, and laughed, huh huh, huh

huh. "Good one, Morey!"

"I'm Linney," said Linney, abandoning her struggle with her hamburger. "Nice to meet you, Palmer." Her voice sounded better than mine, of course. And of course, she said the right thing.

"Hi, Linney," said Palmer.

"Would you like the rest of my shake?" I asked him.

"Rilly? Rilly? What flavor?"

"Vanilla," I said.

"My fave," he said, and grabbed it, sucked through the straw with a big slurping sound. I couldn't stop smiling. I'd gotten rid of the food and made touch-and-exchange-germs contact with a human.

Linney tried to change her expression, but the Mask wasn't fast enough.

Skitty smiled at me, and I was used enough to the expression now to realize I was doing really well.

§§§

The Key to Everything

My special talent was pissing people off. That wasn't the technical term for it, but that was what I was good at. You would think there wouldn't be much demand for this talent. That would be you, wrong again.

On a station like Confetti, where three different alien-to-each-other races came to celebrate their very varied holidays and religious rites, there was a lot of bumping into each other's sore spots. People in the service industries needed to be difficult to irritate. If an administrator wanted to test an employee's capacity to suck up the pain and keep on smiling, hey, enter me.

I dressed in my best I'm-not-going-to-be-here-long-enough-to-take-my-consequences tourist garb, and went to my next job.

The Rikrik were about to arrive in masses for Recombo Night. I went to the Lerva Bar, a place that specialized in Rikrik beverages, comestibles, and behavior-cushioning. Bypassing the hostess, who would have led me into the human section, I went right up to the serving platform, though Rikrik custom dictated that patrons, both human and Rikrik, be led to an exchange nest and wait for a server to approach. A server would only approach when every Rikrik in a nest raised the topmost appendage in unison or when every human in a party did the same.

The bartender didn't flinch or otherwise indicate that she had noticed my bad behavior. I asked her to make me a fruit squash, and she whipped one up and presented it with a smile.

I sipped and grimaced. "This tastes too distil," I

whined. "I want the color a bluer green. The ploorberries are too ripe. Do it over."

Genera, the bartender, was human like me, and unlike me, she had a great fake smile. "So sorry, sentient," she said. She took my drink, poured it into the recycle oubliette, and started making another from scratch.

I leaned back and surveyed the bar. The walls were interlaced trilla vines spangled with glowing flowers, and the ceiling was aflutter with their mirrored leaves, flickering in a soft, constant, artificial wind. Light spots flashed and danced across the floor and walls. Small snaky fliers from Rikrik darted through the upper air. Sometimes they encountered each other, entwined, and fell writhing to the floor, swapping out sections of their bodies in the same process the sentient Rikrik practiced. The air had an acrid taint, the acid tang of too-ripe pineapple.

Just as Genera was about to add the comet spice to the second coming of my beverage, I said, "Wait. A spiktor fell in. I can't drink that."

"I assure you, sentient, we have more than adequate pest control at Lerva," she said, her voice unruffled. "We do not host spiktors here." However, she poured that drink out as well and built me another.

I could have gone for yet another sting, but the drink smelled great, and I was hungry, so I took it from her. It was so good—all the proportions of flavors perfect, a bouquet on my tongue—I could not bring myself to complain. I felt I'd already stretched my stress application enough. I even complimented her on the drink. The faint telltale lines of irritation at the corners of her eyes smoothed away.

Three Rikrik rolled into the bar. Their bodies were like uneven tubes, with accordion pleats in them, randomly bulging here and there, with parts in various colors—one was red, pink, chartreuse, and orange; another green and yellow; the third blush, lavender, and blue; all the results of previous recombos. Their tool-using limbs were highly flexible, and wrapped around them as they rolled. They burbled like Terran guinea pigs.

"Greetings, sentients, and welcome to Lerva," Genera said in passable Rikrik. "How may I serve you?"

"Do us the honor of the first slice," said the three of them in unison, only each voice was half a tone flatter than the last. The clash of harmonics drilled into my skull.

"It would be my honor," Genera said.

The Rikrik writhed and rolled into one of the nests, then raised their topmost appendages. Genera got out a shining metal box almost two meters long and laid it on the bar. She pumped current through it, then opened it and extracted a tool, the Key to Everything. Its narrow blade was a conglomerate of emerald, sapphire, and ruby.

"Are you a registered slicer?" I asked her.

"Of course."

"Have you done this before?"

"Sentient, it has been my honor to perform this duty for seven Recombo Nights now. I trained under the great slicer Bitterwind. Worry not."

I chugged the rest of my fruit squash, a disgrace when true appreciation would have me sip once every few minutes and savor each sip for some time before essaying another. "You don't want to do that."

She lifted the blade, which was almost as long

as she was tall. Her smile didn't fade even then, when I challenged her in the rudest possible manner.

The Rikrik waved their appendages again, more agitated this time. "We await our first slice," one of them said, which was out of ordinary, too. They always spoke in unison, especially this close to a recombination.

"You endanger my guests, sentient," Genera said quietly to me. "They are losing synchronicity."

"I need another squash," I said.

"Sentient, I need your patience," she said. She gave me a stern look, the lines by her eyes etched deep now. She stepped around the bar and went to the nest.

"Show me you are aligned," she said to the Rikrik.

Three appendages rose and wagged. One moved a little more slowly than the other two.

"Retune, honored guests," she said.

I wandered over to where she stood in the slicer position, her feet on the mosaic of a fractured circle, watching the Rikrik, who rolled back and forth, tapping each other with their lower appendages.

"While they're doing that, could you make me another squash?" I asked. "This time, I want one with coco water in it. And stirred so the layers separate only slightly."

"Sentient, please step back. You are interrupting a sacred rite."

Three appendages rose from the nest and moved in perfect unison.

Genera lifted the blade and sliced it down into three bodies at once. She carved again, lifting sections from all three of the Rikrik with the flat of the jewel blade. She flicked the blade. The sections, still dripping the faintly blue blood of Rikrik circulatory systems, rose in the air. With a swift strike, she drove the sections down, each into a different body from the one it had begun in. Her movements were deft and assured. She toed a button that closed the top over the nest and initiated the healing mist. The Rikrik would spend a few hours in hibernation and integration and emerge later, their characters and bodies slightly altered.

Genera was a slicing genius, a pleasure to watch as she worked. Her next move flowed from the others she had finished. Later, she would claim it had been an accident, and on the playback it looked accidental as well, but nobody as skilled as she makes that kind of mistake.

"Hey, Pala," said a voice with bubbles in it.

I groaned and pressed my hand to my belly.

I was lying in the usual bed at ReVive. My usual tender, a Zeloglob named Stasha, waved her eye stalks at me. "How many eyes do you see?" she asked.

"Three?" Stasha had seven eye stalks. She could retract them at will.

"Three is correct!" Stasha's eyes danced around each other in dizzy-making spirals. "Another successful revival!" she aspirated.

"I don't feel right."

"Well, you won't. No telling whether you ever will. Look at this." Her upper arm, frilled with finger stalks, gestured toward my stomach, and one of her other arms moved forward, holding a magnifying mirror. She used an eye stalk to gauge where I was looking so she could position the mirror within my view.

My belly, which had formerly been a uniform

brown, had a narrow diamond band of new colors in it: lavender, rose, and green, like a small kite just to the left of my navel. I lifted a hand and brushed it across my new and alien body part. There were no discernable seams or separations. Perfect blend, the result of skillful slicing.

I groaned again. No wonder my stomach was roiling.

"She's been arrested, but she claims innocence. She did it with the Key to Everything. We had no idea that could work across species."

"Will I—will it settle?"

"There's still activity at the wound site, heat and fleshknit. It seems to be integrating. Nobody's sure what the upshot will be. The boss has put you into retirement so we can study you. That's temporary if you recover all right. For now, you belong to me and Malmurum." All seven of her eye stalks focused on my face, hungry, I thought, to read my next expression. Stasha was obsessed with human emotional reactions to stress. She loved studying them, which made her a perfect recovery agent at ReVive. She was a poster child for schadenfreude.

I gave her the satisfaction of another groan.

The problem with being a professional irritant is that sometimes you do manage to irritate people beyond sense. They break. They fracture. You discover where they don't work by pushing them past their limits.

My job came with the best worker's compensation insurance in existence. Not many people rose to my level of inciting ire. The bosses always brought me back after one of my successful failures to accurately gauge someone's limits.

This time, though, I wasn't sure whether I'd be

able to get back in the game. Ever since the incident, I've been hearing burbling voices whispering just too softly for me to make out the words. They are not quite tuned to each other. Their harmonics clash at the edge of my consciousness, and I'm having trouble focusing.

Pisses me off.

§§§

First Faces

I love October. That's when I can wear the mask and people ask the right kinds of questions, like who made it, where'd I get it, and what it's supposed to be.

The answers vary according to my mood. I never tell the truth—an ancestor made it, it's come down from mother to oldest daughter for more than two hundred years, and it's not what it looks like but what it does that matters.

If I wear the mask other times of year, people ask, "What is that ugly thing, and why is it on your face?" I've come up with answers: "It's better than my real face," or "I'm having a bad face day," or, "It's a face-hugging alien and it's sucking out my brain. Back off before it jumps to your face." If I say things like that, though, folks think I'm peculiar.

The inside of the mask is hairy, like the outside of a coconut shell. It smells like the beach—salt air, tanning oil. Once I put it on, I don't notice the rough surface, and the smell is faint. Green crystal ovals cover the eyeholes. They're what I love about the mask. When I look through the eyes, the world's transformed. Intangible beings drift here and there. Plants have extra shadows made of light. Animals trail second selves.

And people? People wear their first faces over their second ones, the faces they really are, not the faces they want you to see.

Many of my relationships change in October, altered by what I see.

I wore the mask to the office Halloween party. The other secretary, Helen, who was dressed as a sexy red devil woman, said, "Penny, again? This is the third year in a row you've worn the same thing! Penny Dreadful! I hate looking at that awful, twisted face! Why don't you get a new costume?" Her first face was pinched, narrow-eyed and sharp-nosed, unlike her gentle, rounded second face, but it wore an extra-wide smile when she thought something was funny. I liked Helen.

I modeled my new tiger-and-jungle tattoo sleeves, and the giant bejeweled spider ring. "These are new."

"Steps in the right direction," said Helen, "but still with the same black wispy witch costume? And that horrible matted-hair wig?" She wrinkled her nose.

I shrugged. "Where's the boss?"

She pointed a red-claw-tipped finger. "Came as a demon this year, so it's like every day in the office. He brought a new girlfriend."

Mr. Jimson's first face, a leering lecher with too-large features, hovered above a muscular body in a blue-black body stocking, with black bat wings, a pointy tail, black leather pants, and black knee-high leather boots. He held a red trident in his left hand. His right hand gripped the wrist of something I had never seen before.

Its body looked misty through the mask's eyes, shifting from fox to snake to sprite, its only solid part the limb the boss grasped.

"Girlfriend?" I asked Helen faintly.

"Doesn't she look like some poor Eastern European girl a Russian mobster shipped over here to sell into prostitution?" Helen said.

"Hey, Penny," said one of the cubicle slaves, Cliff, dressed this year as a Roman gladiator, but with the same first face as last year, a cross between a rat and a weasel. "How about a kiss?"

"You'd kiss that mouth?" Helen said. "You must be drinking."

Cliff waved his can of Coors.

"Sorry, Cliff. Gotta go." I headed toward the boss. At office parties, he pretended to be jolly and friendly and caring. It was creepy, but better than his everyday self. He expected everyone to greet him and thank him for the party. Once I got that chore out of the way, I could focus on studying everyone I worked with. On Halloween, with the mask's help, I got enough juicy details about my coworkers to keep me going the rest of the year.

"Yikes! An evil witch!" said the boss when I approached. Then he guffawed. "It's you, isn't it, Penny? Looking better than usual!"

"Thanks, Mr. Jimson." He made the same joke every year. Maybe he meant it, though. I was grateful he didn't look at me twice on normal days. My clothes covered my body in neutral colors. I left my face naked and kept my hair short to discourage his interest, and it worked. He treated me like a useful robot. Better than he treated Helen. "Who's your friend?" I asked.

"This is Morana Bosko. She's with Kowalski Toolcraft. She's never been to a Halloween party before."

Up close, I still couldn't see Morana's second face. Her first face looked like a fox, then a cat, then a fairy. The fairy face smiled. "What are you?" she asked. Her voice was warm, deep, and smoky.

"I'm a secretary," I said. What was she?

"Fascinating," she said, with just a hint of accent. She wrenched free of the boss's grip and slipped her arm through mine. "Let us get beverages together."

The boss reached for her, but she evaded him. Her arm was cold, and she smelled like wood smoke and nettles. My mouth went dry. Cold gripped me.

I had seen many things through the mask's eyes, but none scared me more than Morana did.

She led me toward the refreshment tables, then past them and down the hall.

She pushed me into the reception room, where Helen and I worked during the day. Our desks stood abandoned, the lights off except for a nightlight. The rogue jade plant loomed in the corner, its many-leaved shadow huge and menacing. "The mask," Morana said. "Will you show it to me?"

"Um, no?" I stepped back. Her hand on my arm felt like metal pliers.

She reached for the mask. I turned my head.

Her hand dropped. "What would convince you to let me examine it?"

"Tell me what you are."

"Ah," she said. "So that's what it does. I am not human. More than that, I will not say."

"What do you want with me?"

"Only a look through your mask's eyes."

I took off my mask. To my daytime eyes, Morana looked like an exotic but beautiful woman, with a broad, pale face, large dark eyes, and a wide, thin-lipped mouth. Her hair was dark gray, worn loose. Her dress was gray-green, with silver woven into it. She plucked the mask from my hand and put it over her face.

I'd never looked in a mirror while wearing it. It was like fissured tree bark, the crystal lenses like sap blisters, the mouth a protruding O, the nose hooked. She stared at me. "Ah," she said, her voice muffled. "Yes. Very good." She took the mask off, and then she kissed me.

My mother had never told me why we had the mask, who made it, or where it came from. Maybe she didn't know that those who wear the mask have certain unusual skills.

I work for Morana Soulreaper now. I wear the mask while working.

Now I know what to look for.

§§§

Don't Answer

Tonight is the night they come back.

My parents locked me and my younger sister India in our room every year until this one. Now they say I'm old enough to sit in the living room, to hear the knock on the door, the cries and whispers at the windows. My sister is up in our bedroom all alone, with a plywood board nailed over the window for the night. She has her iPad with the Wi-Fi disabled, and a stockpile of snack foods and decaffeinated beverages. She's not allowed to look at news tonight. Dad put the camping toilet in our room, just like last year.

Mom closed all the living room curtains, the gauze ones and the heavy winter curtains. Usually light leaks into the windows from the streetlight outside. Tonight the only light in the room is from the candles Mom lit on ceramic plates around the room. She put six on top of the piano and two on the coffee table. Everything's golden and grim. It's spookier than if she turned on the regular lights.

Dad hands me a mug of hot chocolate. It has marshmallows in it. I sip. It's my favorite fall drink, and usually I only get it when I'm very good. I say, "Wait. I thought I was old enough for tonight. Isn't this a kid drink?"

"Abida, you're a tweener now," says Mom.

"What does that even mean?"

A knock sounds on the door.

"Shh," whispers Dad.

I drink. The chocolate whispers warmth and comfort, spreading sweet and dark across my tongue. I savor it and wait for Dad to get the door.

The knock sounds again, louder this time. I put

down my mug and walk toward the door.

"Don't answer," Mom whispers.

"Is it Kevin?" I say that aloud, and then I hear, all along the walls, the whispers and murmurs of many people outside.

"Mom, it's me," says Kevin's voice through the door. Kevin. My twin brother, who died last year. My left side is always cold because he's not there where he belongs.

"It's not," Mom whispers.

"Abida. It's me. Let me in. I just want to see you again."

"Kevin!" I run to the front door and grab the doorknob.

Dad grasps my arm, but I unlock the deadbolt and turn the knob before he can stop me.

The door eases open an inch, two inches, three, and I see Kevin. He's not solid, more a space outlined in blue light, but his face has the same half smile we turned on each other when we shared a joke without speaking it aloud. My whole body aches from missing him. I reach for the mental touch we used to have all the time, one of the other things I miss constantly.

My mind touches something arctic cold. It hurts. I stick to it as though I licked a frozen flagpole. A tiny spiral of warmth, an orange fingerprint, is melting through the utter ice. The pattern and the color feel familiar, the cheery glow of my life before Kevin died. I reach out—

Dad slams the door and locks it. His arm wraps roughly around my shoulders. He jerks me back toward the living room. "Do you know what you just did?" he whispers.

"Kevin," I whisper.

"It's not Kevin." He sets me in front of him and

shakes my shoulders. "Abida. It's not Kevin. Kevin's gone. You know that."

I don't know that. I just saw him. Felt him.

Not him. But a version of him. Better than nothing. Better than the last half-dead year, where I had zombied through my life, alive only in the art of remembering all the ways Kevin wasn't there anymore.

The door rattles. The deadbolt turns. The door eases open a crack. One inch, two, three. Something green and eerie oozes in, spreads across the hardwood floor, rolling toward us on a low, bubbling, cloudy tide.

"Too late," Mom whispers.

She and Dad embrace. They close their eyes as the green touches their shoes and sizzles.

I glance up and think of India, locked in the room upstairs, a blanket along the crack of the door to keep things out. Snacks. Beverages. A toilet. Maybe in the morning she'll be able to make enough noise to get someone to come and let her out.

I kneel and reach toward the green with my hand, toward Kevin with my mind.

I feel him. I'm sure.

I'm not sure.

§§§

Just Today

My best friend, Ben, is dead. We still hang. Not too many other people can see or hear him—just little kids and animals, and an occasional weirdo, so Ben is kind of stuck with me, which works for me. We do most things together.

I was walking to middle school on a brilliant blue fall day, the kind where the light was so sharp it almost cut, and the orange, red, and yellow leaves flamed like stained glass with the sun behind them.

In the grassy, tree-dotted park to my left, people played Frisbee golf. Chains clinked as they sunk their putts. On the road to my right, cars growled and snorted past. I crunched acorns under my feet on the sidewalk, like popping bubble wrap, and kicked up the spicy smell of downed leaves whenever I came to a wind-driven drift of them. I loved autumn.

But today was Halloween. Halloween, the one-year anniversary of Ben's death, when I'd held him in my arms after the hit-and-run driver drove away, leaving us in the dark in the middle of the street, candy scattered on the pavement, and Ben's body too smashed up to survive.

Today, Ben drifted from treetop to treetop, startling rafts of birds into flight. "Hey, I feel like I'm on a pirate ship," he called from the top of a bright yellow sycamore. "In the crow's nest!" Three black crows flapped away from him. "Everywhere I look there's an ocean of leaves, all colors. I wish you could see this, Rissa."

My nemesis, Ethan Arlen, jumped out from behind a white-trunked tree and grabbed my shoulders. "Aaaiiee!" I jerked.

Usually, Ben kept a lookout for Ethan and warned me to hide before I got caught. But not today. Today Ben was distracted by pirate ship trees.

"Gotcha," Ethan said, employing his masterful power of overstating the obvious.

I'd never been able to figure out why Ethan hated me. My fatness? My thrift store clothes? My loud mouth? My tortoise-shell cat's-eye glasses? There were lots of other kids he could torture more easily—I was no lightweight, and I knew how to punch.

Mom said Ethan was secretly in love with me. Gag.

I brought my fists up. Ethan was a hulking, shambling monster of an eighth grader. I was big, but he was twice my size. His face was close to mine as he breathed his swoon-inducing garlic breath into my face to weaken me. Usually his shaggy, dirt-brown hair hung down to hide his face, but I had seen what was under it, and that was one of the creepy things about Ethan. He was actually handsome.

Ethan dropped his hands from my shoulders to my wrists, squeezing them so hard I thought my hands would fall off.

"Whatcha want?" I said. The sun was too bright. The birds sang too loudly. My wrists ached, and I felt the deadness settle in me, the knowledge that if I fought, Ethan would just hurt me worse, so why bother. Been there, done that, got the I HATE BULLIES T-shirt.

"Whatcha got?" he asked. He gripped both my wrists in one of his giant hands, and pawed at my backpack with the other.

"I'm sorry, Rissa, I forgot to watch." Ben danced

around both of us.

Ethan pulled my lunch out of my pack and stuffed it in his coat pocket. He dug deeper and found the bag of chocolate pumpkin muffins I'd packed for Mrs. Larrabee's art class, my favorite class. It was hard for Ethan to open the bag one-handed, but he managed it, and took a deep sniff. "What is this shit?" he asked. He dropped the bag on the ground and stomped on it.

I screeched. I couldn't help it. I'd spent a lot of time last night making those, and skipped some of my homework to do it.

Ethan shoved his face right up close to mine. "Quiet!" he said. "Shut up, or I'll give you something to cry about!"

I had a sense of deja vu. I'd heard Ethan's big brother Kyle say the same thing to him a couple years earlier, when Ethan and I were both smaller. Kyle was even bigger then than Ethan was now, and he used to fall on top of Ethan during recess. It always looked like an accident, but sometimes Ethan ended up with a broken bone. Ethan was more relaxed now that Kyle, after flunking eighth grade once, had finally moved on to high school.

I shut up.

Ben jumped on Ethan's back, grabbed his head, and tried to shake it. He'd done this before and it never worked, but unlike me, he kept trying things that didn't work.

This time something was different.

"Huh?" Ethan said. He shook his head and looked around.

"Hey, it's working!" Ben tugged on Ethan's hair. His hands didn't really grab handfuls, but some of the hair stuck up in weird, staticky tufts.

"What?" said Ethan, eyes wide, face pale.

Ben and I had spent hours watching ghost movies and experimenting to see if he could improve his grasp on reality. Nothing helped. When he tried to grab anything, his hands went through it. He couldn't move stuff with his mind. He could barely make a cold spot for me to walk through. This was the first time he'd succeeded in affecting matter.

"Take that, you giant jerk!" Ben yelled, squeezing at Ethan's huge neck.

"What? That tickles!" Ethan said. He let go of me to scratch his neck. I punched him in the stomach, then turned and ran.

I thought maybe I got away, but after a pause, he came. "Rissa, hey, wait. Rissa, wait," he yelled as I neared the school. "Wait! It's me, Ben!" he called just as I veered past the Girl Club, the queens of eighth grade, who always gave me a hard time if I let them. I slowed, safe among chattering kids, figuring the presence of others was some protection.

Ethan puffed up to me and brushed the hair out of his face. He smiled. I'd never seen Ethan smile, though I'd seen him sneer plenty of times. "It's me," he said. "Ben. I kind of slipped inside him." He didn't sound like Ethan. He dug my lunch out of his pocket and handed it back to me, something else Ethan had never done before.

I stared into his eyes. His eyes looked the same, iced-tea brown, not green like Ben's. But he wasn't hurting me, so I tried a smile of my own.

"Maybe it's just today," he said.

"Today's good," I said.

§§§

The Power of the Cocoon

The living room had the usual appearance of Christmas aftermath, as though a herd of many-armed elephants had rushed through, grabbed anything wrapped in paper, ripped the paper off, tossed it on the floor, then stomped on it. The multi-colored twinkly lights on the Christmas tree reflected from scraps of foil paper and the firework bursts of discarded metallic ribbon.

Emma's older sister Alice had carried her new supply of glam clothes and trending devices up to her room. Emma's younger brothers Oliver and Lowell had raced outside with their new Razor electric scooters, leaving the rest of their gifts in staggering stacks by the couch where they had unwrapped them.

Grandma Clare was sitting in the armchair by the fireplace, staring at the torn paper at her feet. Her gifts were tucked neatly into a box on the side table near her chair. She had deployed her knitting needles and was clicking away.

Dad was in the kitchen, frying ham for the afternoon meal. The smell made Emma's stomach growl, despite all the Christmas pancakes she'd eaten before the mad gift-unwrapping scramble of the morning.

Mom, hands on her hips as she stood by the door, looked over the living room and said, "Emma, would you and Gran clean up in here? The cousins are coming in a couple of hours, and I have a lot of things to do before they get here."

"Sure," Emma said.

"Thanks, sweetie." Mom dropped a kiss on Emma's cheek and rushed through the swinging door toward the kitchen.

Emma studied her own stack of gifts. Again this year she hadn't gotten a single thing she'd asked for. She was fifteen. She hadn't gotten what she wanted for Christmas since she'd asked for a Golden Angel Barbie when she was ten. Her favorite Christmas ever.

This year, she had a bunch of useful gifts, including nudges to study from Mom and Dad in the form of educational video games. Ugh. She'd gotten one silvery knit shirt that didn't totally suck. The rest of the gifts were things she'd never use or wear. Even Lowell, her favorite brother, had failed her. He'd bought her a shoot-to-kill video game he would enjoy much more than she would.

Gran put down her knitting needles. "Emma, dear, take your things upstairs and come back down. I've got a secret to show you."

"Oh, boy!" Gran's secrets were the best. Emma took her presents up and dumped them on her bed, then raced back downstairs and pulled a chair over next to Gran's.

"I don't know if you noticed," Gran said, resting her hand on Emma's knee, "but I didn't give you your present yet."

"Oh. No, Gran, I'm sorry. I didn't notice."

"That's fine, dear. I was saving your gift till now. Do you know how special you are?"

Emma felt heat in her cheeks. "You always say that, Gran, but it's not true. Alice is so talented! She has the voice of an angel. Everybody says she should be on *American Idol*. Lowell is the best at any sport he tries, and Oliver is so smart. I'm the brown bird in a family of peacocks."

Gran patted Emma's knee. "You're the one I teach the secrets to," she said.

Emma put her hand over Gran's. "Yes."

"Get out your needles and yarn."

Emma fetched the wickerwork basket where she kept her craft supplies, all things Gran had been teaching her. She pulled out the soft red-and-silver scarf she was knitting. She had about six inches on it so far. "Is this going to help us clean up the room?" she asked.

"Oh, yes. It's the best part of Christmas. I've been saving this secret for you for years now. Get your needles ready."

Emma finished a row and held her needles poised for the next stitch.

"Now," Gran whispered, "use your other eyes to look at the paper. What do you see?"

Emma blinked into the special sight Gran had been teaching her to use. "Oh!" she cried.

The room had turned into a forest of colored threads of light that formed images: heaps of holiday food, fashionable clothes, fantastically ornate toys, electronics—the huge-screen TV Dad had wanted, the bells-and-whistles laptop Mom had wanted, the iPhones all the kids had requested and not gotten—and a boy and girl, holding hands, who looked like Alice and her hoped-for boyfriend Blake, all glowing and idealized, with a taste/fragrance of spice, cocoa, and peppermint that tasted like joy.

"This is the power of the cocoon," Gran whispered. "What enwraps and conceals potential. Until you actually open the gifts, you don't know but that they'll be the most wonderful things you've ever seen or touched or used. Hope soaks into the paper all year, and especially all of December. Our fantasies of joy."

"Oh," Emma whispered. She held out her hand

to a glowing image of her own dream gift, a thirty-six-color box of Prismacolor pencils and a big sketch pad. Gran had been teaching her the power of images, how if you captured an accurate picture of something, you could change it. Cameras didn't quite work—not enough of herself went into the capture to give her power over the image. She was taking drawing classes as her elective this year.

"There hope lies, before us," Gran whispered. "Now, repeat these words after me, and knit it into your project. That locks it up until you want to let it loose again. You can drink it, or nibble on it, or wear it, or send it out to do work for you. Here are the words." Gran taught Emma the secret chant.

They knitted together, murmuring the chant over and over, and stitching dreams into interlocking loops to wear and savor later.

"Fantastic!" Mom said, startling Emma out of bright, tasty wishes.

Emma looked around. The room was clear of paper; only the presents people hadn't put away yet remained of the morning's unwrapping.

Emma stroked the length of scarf across her lap. Warmth wrapped her, and golden light, and the taste of gingerbread and whipped cream lay on her tongue. She shared a smile with Gran.

§§§

Company for the Holidays

"There's nobody else, Aunt Phyllida," my niece Alice said over the phone. "You have to take Sam for Christmas."

"I can't. I absolutely, positively can't," I said. I set down the golden candleholder I was carrying and glanced around my living room. The windows were covered in black velvet curtains, and every surface bore at least one layer of midnight cloth. I had cleaned the fireplace and laid new wood in it. Shadows loved fire.

"He's been at my house for three days, and if he stays any longer, he'll ruin Christmas. Rob and I have been planning this holiday for months, Aunt Phyllida. The girls were so excited about it until Sam came. I can't stand it. We need a good holiday after what happened with Rob's mom."

Rob's mother had died just after Thanksgiving. I hadn't been invited to the funeral. They all thought I was eccentric, and they were right. Couldn't trust me to behave at family events. That's what they thought. They had no idea who I was, what I wanted, who I knew, or who visited me.

"Your family deserves relief from the grief," I said. "Still, I don't think I should have a child in my house over the holiday." Christmas wasn't the problem. It was the winter solstice, which was tonight. I couldn't have a twelve-year-old kid in my house during the Festival of Darks, when shadows came to celebrate the longest night. I didn't think children could survive that intense onslaught of dark energy. It took someone over fifty to host the ceremony. I'd been hosting ShadowFest for ten years, and every year it took a toll on me, though I'd grown out of most of my harshest, most devouring fears. A twelve-year-old would be full of fears—not just the dire fears of childhood, but with the onset of the hormonal teen years, all those social issues to be afraid of. The shadows loved to feed fears and harvest terrors.

"You're the last relative Sam's got," said Alice. "He's already stayed with Aunt Lily and Uncle Tem and Aunt Harriet for various holidays. He's worn out his welcome at all the cousins' houses. My kids think he's creepy and wrong, and Elsa said he spooked her kids, too. It's like that with everybody. You don't have kids to screw up."

"Rub it in." My sisters and brother had given me hella grief about my inability to marry and produce children. All except my favorite sister, Abby, Sam's mother, who had died way too young.

I had last seen Sam when he was eight, at his mother's funeral. He was a small, pale, red-headed boy who didn't look like he would hurt a flea on a fly. He had Abby's gentle nature, I had thought. "Where does he live now?"

"Boarding school. They close over winter break."

"Boarding school," I muttered. For a twelve-year-old? Who did that? We had a large extended family. Why hadn't someone adopted Sam?

"He's been kicked out of two boarding schools already. This is the one for kid criminals."

"What does he do that's so wrong?"

"Nothing anyone can put their finger on. He's just... not right."

"And you want me to take him in."

"You have that guest room with window bars. You could lock him in there for two weeks."

"I could not," I said. I didn't like locking people

up. Although I had set up one of my guest rooms to contain special guests, the ones who shouldn't wander during their visits.... Maybe I could lock the kid up for ShadowFest, anyway.

"Come on, Aunt Phyllida. You've got that big house. Don't you rattle around in there all alone? And on Christmas? Give the kid a break and get yourself some company. It's not like you're allergic to people. You have us all over for the Fourth of July barbecue every year."

"But I'm expecting you then."

"Expect Sam now. I'm bringing him over. I won't take no for an answer."

Sam was still small, pale, and red-headed, only a few inches taller than he'd been at eight. He stared at the porch while Alice glared at me and handed me a battered suitcase. She gave him a one-armed hug and stomped off the porch.

"Come in," I said, and opened the door wider.

He glanced up at me. Glowing amber eyes, furtive. Then he looked away. "Are you sure?"

"What do you mean?"

He hunched his shoulders. "Nobody wants me."

I sighed. "All god's critters got a place in the choir. Come on in and let's get you settled."

Upstairs, he looked at the guest room, then went to the windows and peered at the bars. "Is this jail?"

"Only for tonight. I'm having a party I don't think you should come to. You can move to a different room tomorrow."

"Great," he said and sat on the bed.

I put his suitcase on top of the dresser. "Come on down and look around. You got a tablet or a laptop?"

"No," he said.

"I don't have a television. How do you entertain yourself?"

He shrugged. "I read."

"Good. I have books. You can pick a bunch to keep you company. My guests won't arrive until nightfall. When did you last eat?"

"Breakfast."

"I'll make you some toast or something. What did you do to scare Alice's kids?"

He shrugged. "Nothing. I told them about Krampus."

"Really." I led him downstairs and into the kitchen.

"Why's the living room all black?" he asked.

Why had I forgotten to close the door between the kitchen and the living room? "It's for tonight's party."

"Are the guests dead?" He sounded more interested than afraid.

"Not so much dead as noncorporeal."

"They don't have bodies?"

I smiled. I liked a kid with a big vocabulary. "That's right."

"You know people who don't have bodies?" he whispered. "So do I."

"Oh?" I got down the cookie jar and offered him the soft, chewy ginger cookies I'd made that morning—not what I was planning to give him. Shadows loved spicy smells, so I usually whipped up a few things for their enjoyment. They didn't actually eat physical food, but I ended up throwing away the cookies afterward; they devoured the savor.

"Mostly ghosts," said Sam, and bit into a cookie.

"Really. Would you like to come to a party of

shadows?" If he was spooking every kid he ran into, maybe he already knew how to handle his fears.

His eyes kindled. He nodded.

§§§

Wishmas

A knock sounded on the door.

Arly was sitting at the table with her little brother Sim on her right. Sim was eight, and would have been gone by now if Mama had been normal. Mama sat at the head of the table with the turkey in front of her, and Now-dad sat at the foot of the table with the gravy boat and the mashed potatoes. Across the table from Arly and Sim sat their older sister Kitty, and Granny. Nobody had eaten yet.

"Who could that be?" Mama asked.

"I'll get it," said Sim. He jumped up.

"I don't know that we're ready for visitors just now," said Mama. They had just said grace, and she was about to carve the turkey. Everything smelled so good Arly's mouth watered. She hadn't had anything to eat since breakfast.

While Sim and Now-dad, safely locked in the house, fixed the Wishmas meal, Arly had been out chasing wild boys on her bike. Not like she actually needed boys now, but at some point, her mother had told her, she would need a boy who wasn't her brother, so no practice was wasted. She had tracked three of them to their lairs. They would probably move now that she knew where they lived, but maybe some other boy would move in. So far, Arly had ferreted out twelve lairs in the hills above the village, and she'd found good vantage points to watch their entrances from. She planned to have her pick of boys when the time came for her to find one.

There weren't so many boys around. Most families kicked them out of the house when they were six, and some died when they left home, not trained in ways to survive.

Not everybody could have a boy, but Arly was sure she'd find one when she needed one.

Kitty never chased anybody. She would sure look stupid when her time to catch a boy came.

Sim peered through the peekhole, then glanced back at Mama.

"Who is it?" she asked.

"I don't know," said Sim. "Some boy."

"A boy," said Mama in a thoughtful tone. "Let him in. Arly, set another place at the table. Everybody's welcome on Wishmas Night."

Arly got the extra chair against the wall and set it at the table, moving her own and Sim's place settings along to make room. She got a placemat and silverware and a napkin out of the sideboard.

Sim unchained the door and held it wide, letting in a blast of winter cold.

"Hello," said the stranger in a warm, deep voice. "Is Kitty here?"

"Come on in," Sim said.

The stranger was tall, thin, and raggedy. His boots were scuffed. His jeans had worn spots at the knees. He wore a khaki jacket over a plaid shirt, and a ratty scarf around his neck. His hair was black, his eyes dark, and his skin was the color of gravy. He was the most beautiful boy Arly had ever seen.

Sit by me, she thought. She stood behind her chair and wished as hard as she could.

"Switch places with me, Arly," said Kitty as she rose.

Arly looked at Mama, who nodded.

So much for Wishmas, Arly thought, but she shuffled around the table and took Kitty's seat next to Granny, who smelled of peppermints.

"Kitty, introduce us to your boy," said Mama.

"Everyone, this is Trevis," said Kitty. "He's not

my boy yet. He wanted to meet my family. If y'all are nice, maybe he'll be my boy."

"Ooh, Kitty. You're giving him a choice?" said Granny.

"I am," said Kitty. "Trevis? Would you like to sit?"

"Sure," said Trevis. He sat next to Kitty, with little Sim to his right. "So long since I've been with a family on Wishmas Night," he said.

"Where'd you come from?" Arly asked.

"Up the river," said Trevis. He looked at her. His eyes were so warm and dark. He smiled. Most boys didn't smile at her. They just ran.

Arly had actually caught a boy that afternoon, a small one, who had whimpered when she landed on top of him. He'd smelled sour, and he'd been covered with dirt and scratches. He'd struggled at first, making little grunting sounds, but then he quieted and just looked up at her. So pale and skinny and scared. Too small. She had rolled off him and let him go.

Trevis looked clean, and he didn't stink.

Mama carved the turkey and placed slices on plates, then passed them down the table. Now-dad got the first plate. He was a good dad, handy around the house, knew how to cook and mend, glad to have a good place to live. Arly liked him better than the last three dads.

Trevis stared at the turkey on the plate Kitty put in front of him. He licked his lip.

He looked pretty thin, Arly thought, but he had manners. He waited until everybody had some food and Mama started eating before he took a bite. He used a knife and fork better than Sim did.

"How did Kitty find you?" Arly asked Trevis after everybody'd eaten something.

"I found her down by the river where my raft came ashore," he said.

The river! Kitty was always at the river. Most days, fishing.

"She invited me to dinner," he said. "Said I'd see what a nice household you had, and I could decide whether to stay. Food's great."

Imagine Kitty finding this boy and letting him go. How stupid was that?

But he came back.

"And you folk seem nice," said Trevis. "May I stay awhile?"

"Certainly," said Mama. "Will you work your way?"

"Yes, ma'am."

Arly thought of the chains in the basement. She'd been planning to use them on any wild boy she caught until she could tame him. How had Kitty found a tame one?

Wishmas. Wishmas. It was always somebody else's wish that came true, Arly thought, scowling, and served herself another scoop of potatoes.

§§§

Solstice Cakes

I'm not the one who should get the family recipe. It has passed from mother to daughter for more generations than anybody can count, and I'm a son, not a daughter. But my three sisters didn't have the vision to read the writing on the family recipe page, and I did, so Mom was stuck with training me to make the solstice cakes.

I was seventeen, and looking forward to running away to the Western Culinary Institute next year, partly to get away from Dad, who said these things that sounded like compliments but weren't, like, "Nice quiche, Zach. Very flavorful. Who knew you had it in you?"

I'd been interested in cooking since I was nine, so he should know I had it in me by now.

He said things like that about my songwriting, too. "What a cute little jingle. Maybe you could write songs for ads." When I heard that, something inside me crumpled like paper smashed in a fist. I stopped playing my songs for the family after that. I took my guitar out to the woods and recorded my songs on my phone instead, and only shared them with my sister Mora, who smiled or cried at the right times and always told me they were great.

When Mom told Dad at dinner that I was going to get the family recipe, his cheeks flushed. He stared at me from under lowered brows, his mouth straight. His shoulders sagged. Then he got up and left the room.

He didn't even mock me about it.

On the winter solstice, Mom and I got together in the kitchen. We washed and put all the dishes away and scrubbed off the stove and the inside of the oven. Then Mom smudged with a white sage bundle she'd put together earlier in the season, when she had time to go to the desert and gather the sage, and I used a fan to direct the fragrant smoke to every corner. We'd done this together before. We'd cooked and baked together since I was nine. She had taught me most of what I knew.

When it came time to make the solstice cakes, we stared at each other. She'd always had it in her head that this was only for girls, and I'd believed that all my life, too. We stood on either side of the butcher-block table, a mixing bowl in front of each of us, and ingredients in a line down the middle of the table. The vellum recipe page lay sideways so we could both see it.

I glanced at the recipe, then looked at the things laid out between us. "Which one is the starlight? How do you even collect that?"

Mom swallowed, then said, "There's a special sieve. This is the starlight." She touched a small glass jar with a lid on it. "It's tricky to work with. If you're not careful, it'll escape."

"I'll watch what you do," I said.

She bit her lip and nodded. "We start with the clover flour." She picked up a cookie tin and a measuring cup. I grabbed my measuring cup. She opened the tin, which was full of green powder.

"Jeeze, I thought that was a spelling mistake," I said. "It's not flowers? You really powdered clover?"

"Yes, as it was and is and always will be." The words rolled out like a prayer. Then she blinked and looked at me. "Was, is, and always will be" had changed this year.

She let out a breath and dipped her measuring

cup into the green powder. I copied her.

We worked without speaking. We both studied the recipe, and I watched Mom to see what she'd pick up next, then copied her actions. "Where do you keep these ingredients between solstices?" I asked her.

"There's a secret door in the basement. The hidden pantry is down there. Oh, heavens, I'll have to teach you how to collect everything." The despair in her voice knifed my heart.

"I didn't exactly sign up for this," I said. My voice shook. Dad was already distancing himself from me even more because of this. Why couldn't Mora or Beth or Kalla have been worthy? Stupid sisters. There were three of them, and none of them—

"Yes. I'm sorry, Zach. I'm just worried whether this will work, and if it doesn't.... Well, we need this to work."

Solstice cakes kept us well, kept pests of all kinds away from our bodies and our house. When everybody else was down with flu and colds, we were fine. The houses on either side of ours had been burgled, but no one ever stole from us. When I was ten, I'd seen Brad Gates, the school bully, stare at me, then look away and beat up other kids for lunch money. Boys who went into the military in our family always came home. Girls married men who treated them well. No one had died in childbirth in the recorded history of our family.

"Let's just get it done," I said.

When we had the batter in the cake pans, Mom recited a chant in the Other Language over her three cakes. I listened while she said it, watched the words on the parchment, but they were blurred and confusing. She hadn't taught me the Other

Language. She had been saving it for when one of the girls would show the spark.

But I had the spark.

I closed my eyes and memorized sounds.

When Mom finished, I repeated the chant. I didn't look at her while I did it, afraid I'd stumble over a word, though my verbal memory was good. I could hear a song once and sing it.

The words in my mouth had flavors: caramel, citrus, nutmeg, anise, peppermint, the green of grass stems, fresh bread. The tastes didn't mix, but happened one after the other. With the last word, a taste lay on my tongue like morning, sweet, fresh, hopeful. I swallowed it and looked at Mom.

She smiled.

We put the cakes in the oven, and while they baked, filling the house with that warm, spicy cake scent, we gathered up the leftover ingredients.

When we took the cakes out, mine looked as brown and appetizing as Mom's. I leaned over and sniffed. They all smelled so good.

How were we going to find out whether mine worked? Half the family would eat my cakes and maybe be unprotected until the next solstice.

Mom held her hands over the cakes and said a short chant. All the cakes emitted an orange glow. Her smile started small, then stretched wide. She pulled me into a hug. "Perfect child," she whispered.

After they cooled, we took the cakes out and set them on the dining room table, then called the girls and Dad. Mom lit the solstice candles, and I got a tray of glasses of water from the kitchen.

Dad stood by his chair at the head of the table and looked at the cakes. "I can't tell which ones are real," he said.

"They're all real," said Mom.

"Which are Zach's?"

"Does it matter?"

"I want one of Zach's," he said. He looked at my sisters.

Mora got mad. "Dad!"

I didn't get it, and then I did. He thought my cakes wouldn't work, and he would save one of the rest of us from a defective cake. And Mora figured it out.

My cheeks prickled with sudden cold. Crumpled paper in my chest again. Mom gripped my shoulder, and I remembered the tastes of the chant in my mouth, and the warmth of our kitchen, and the moment when all the cakes glowed. I smoothed my hands down my chest, across my ribs, uncrumpling what was crushed.

What Dad said didn't help. I didn't have to listen anymore.

"Eat," said Mom.

We all sat down and ate. Sweet ginger spice, moist cake, and the flavor of safety.

After we ate, Mom showed me the way to open the secret door in the basement.

The hidden pantry had lots of shelves, and the light in it was like foxfire. Bunches of drying herbs hung from the ceiling. Labeled bottles, jars, boxes, and twists of paper crowded the shelves. Some of the contents in the jars glowed with their own light. I went to one shelf and read labels. "Bottled lightning?" I whispered. "Cats' shadows? Baby's breath?"

"Oh, Zach. I have so much to teach you." Mom handed me a beat-up leather-bound book from among a clutch of books on one of the shelves.

I let it fall open and found a recipe for "Diverting Attention Powder." "Take one pinch of butterfly wing powder and three pinches of mystery...."

"Have you ever tried this one?" I asked Mom.

She glanced at it. "That's a good one." She handed me a white feather. "Mark the place."

I set the feather between the pages and closed the book with a little fluff sticking out the top. I took a deep breath. The air was redolent of spices and flavors I had never smelled or tasted before. I was already imagining what I could make with them.

§§§

About the Author

Over the past thirty-odd years, Nina Kiriki Hoffman has sold adult and YA novels, short story collections, and more than 300 short stories. Her works have been finalists for the World Fantasy, Mythopoeic, Sturgeon, Philip K. Dick, and Endeavour awards. Her fiction has won a Stoker and a Nebula Award.

A collection of her short stories, *Permeable Borders*, was published in 2012 by Fairwood Press.

Nina does production work for the *Magazine of Fantasy & Science Fiction*. She teaches writing through Lane Community College. She lives in Eugene, Oregon.

For a list of Nina's publications, go to: http://ofearna.us/books/hoffman.html.

Connect with the Author

You can connect with the Nina Kiriki Hoffman through Facebook.

Other Nina Kiriki Hoffman Titles

You can find the following titles online.

Short Fiction:

"Trophy Wives," by Nina Kiriki Hoffman

"Family Tree" by Nina Kiriki Hoffman

"Escapes" by Nina Kiriki Hoffman

"The Ghosts of Strangers" by Nina Kiriki Hoffman

"Ghost Hedgehog" by Nina Kiriki Hoffman

"How I Came to Marry a Herpetologist" by Nina Kiriki Hoffman

"The Weight of Wishes" by Nina Kiriki Hoffman

"Key Signatures" by Nina Kiriki Hoffman

"Haunted Humans" by Nina Kiriki Hoffman

"Zombies for Jesus" by Nina Kiriki Hoffman

"Fast Wedded to the Ground" by Nina Kiriki Hoffman

"A Wolf in Holy Places" by Nina Kiriki Hoffman

"The Dangers of Touch" by Nina Kiriki Hoffman

"Airborn" by Nina Kiriki Hoffman

"Surreal Estate" by Nina Kiriki Hoffman

"Antiquities: Five Stories set in Ancient Worlds" by Nina Kiriki Hoffman

"Wild Talents: Three Short Stories" by Nina Kiriki Hoffman

"Faint Heart, Foul Lady" and "Night Life" by Nina Kiriki Hoffman

"The Skeleton Key" and "Bright Streets of Air" by Nina Kiriki Hoffman

The Other Side Secret by Nina Kiriki Hoffman

"Rags, Riches, and a Dragon: Three Fairy Tales" by Nina Kiriki Hoffman

"Meet in Fear and Wonder: Four Science Fiction Stories" by Nina Kiriki Hoffman

"Savage Breasts and Other Misbehaving Body Parts" by Nina Kiriki Hoffman

"One Day at the Central Convenience Mall" by Nina Kiriki Hoffman

Books

The Spirit in the Clay: A Novelet in the Chapel Hollow/Silent Strength of Stones Universe

Fairy Infestation: A Short Story in the LaZelle Family Magic series

The Silent Strength of Stones (Chapel Hollow

Series) (novel) by Nina Kiriki Hoffman

The Thread that Binds the Bones (Chapel Hollow Series) (novel) by Nina Kiriki Hoffman

Spirits that Walk in Shadow (Chapel Hollow Series) (novel) by Nina Kiriki Hoffman

A Fistful of Sky (LaZelle Family Magic Series) (novel) by Nina Kiriki Hoffman

Fall of Light (LaZelle Family Magic series) (novel) by Nina Kiriki Hoffman

Past the Size of Dreaming (Haunted House Series) (novel) by Nina Kiriki Hoffman

Permeable Borders (short story collection) by Nina Kiriki Hoffman